Cherokee Folktales

Grace Lalrinpari Hauzel

Published by Gumby Publishers, 2023.

Published by Gumby Publishers,
36 Saint John's Place
Freeport 11520-4618
New York, USA

Airhub 1425, UBX 6 Poyle Trading Estate,
Colndale Road, Colnbrook
Slough SL30AA
Berkshire, United kingdom

First Edition: March, 2023

Cherokee folklore is a rich blend of oral traditions, rituals, and myths that are the foundation of Cherokee culture. The stories from Cherokee mythology and folklore tell the story of how the Cherokee people came to be and how their traditions have been passed down through generations.

Preface

In the vast tapestry of human history, the ancient Cherokee nation of North America weaved a rich and enchanting fabric of myths, legends, and folktales. Across generations, these captivating narratives were passed down from elders to the young, carrying with them the timeless wisdom and cultural heritage of these proud and resilient people.

In "Cherokee Folktales," we embark on a journey through the mystical landscapes of Cherokee mythology, where the boundaries between the natural world and the supernatural blur. Within these pages, you will encounter a world where animals hold sacred significance, where the spirits of ancestors and deities weave intricate tales of creation, and where the forces of nature intertwine with the destinies of human beings.

The Cherokee people believed that every living being, be it human or animal, shared a profound interconnectedness. From the trickster Rabbit to the revered Wolf, each creature played a unique role in the cosmic symphony of existence. Through these stories, we witness how the Cherokees close relationship with nature not only shaped their cultural practices but also reflected their deep respect and gratitude for the Earth and its inhabitants.

As the embers of time glow brighter, we delve into the heart of Cherokee folklore to learn the lessons taught by the legendary figures of Kana'tï and Tsul'kălû', and the enigmatic powers of the Little Deer. We explore the ancient rituals and ceremonies that seek harmony with nature and safeguard the delicate balance between the human and animal realms.

While the myths enchant with their fantastical elements, they also hold a mirror to the struggles, beliefs, and aspirations of the Cherokee people. Their profound understanding of the cycles of life, death, and rebirth offer insight into their spiritual practices and the sacred connection with their ancestors.

The retelling of these timeless tales honors the oral tradition that has preserved Cherokee culture for generations. Through the expert narration of these cherished stories, we aim to carry forward the legacy of the Cherokee nation and share their enduring wisdom with readers of all ages and backgrounds.

As we embark on this odyssey through the heart of Cherokee folktales, we invite you to immerse yourself in the vibrant world of myth and magic, where the spirits of the past converge with the present, and where the wisdom of an ancient people illuminates the path to a harmonious coexistence with nature and all living beings.

May these tales awaken the spirit of wonder and ignite the flame of understanding, fostering an appreciation for the profound cultural heritage of the Cherokee people, a legacy that continues to inspire and resonate across the ages.

Grace Lalrinpari Hauzel

About The Author

Grace Lalrinpari Hauzel is an enthusiastic budding writer who has been writing short stories and poetries since she was 6 years old. She manifested her views on life, emphasizing the enigmatic and arduous journey which are often thought provoking. Grace writes about nature, human emotions and divine love, using human love as an allegory. Grace is notorious for being a sleepyhead, most importantly a blithesome person. Her literary skills have gained recognition and have been awarded various awards.

How The World Was Made

The Earth is likened to a vast floating island surrounded by water, suspended at each of its four cardinal points by cords attached to a solid rock firmament above. According to a belief, when the world becomes old and weary, people will perish, the cords will break, and the Earth will sink into the ocean, returning everything to water. The indigenous people, particularly the Indians, are fearful of this eventuality.

In the ancient times when the world was submerged in water, the animals resided in a crowded place above called Gălûñ'lătĭ, situated beyond an arch. Curious about what lay beneath the water, they sent Dâyuni'sĭ, the little water-beetle known as "Beaver's Grandchild," to explore. After searching in vain for a solid resting place on the water's surface, the beetle dove to the bottom and retrieved soft mud. This mud eventually grew and spread to become the island we now call Earth. To secure the Earth, it was anchored to the sky with four cords, but nobody remembers who accomplished this feat.

Initially, the Earth was flat, soft, and wet. The animals were eager to descend, so they dispatched various birds to find a dry spot, but none could land and returned to Gălûñ'lătĭ. Finally, they sent the Great Buzzard, the ancestor of all present-day buzzards, to prepare the Earth for them. The buzzard flew low over the Earth, and wherever its wings struck the ground, valleys formed, and where they turned up again, mountains emerged. Concerned that the Earth would be entirely covered in mountains, they called the buzzard back, but the Cherokee region remained abundant in mountains.

When the Earth was dry, the animals descended but encountered darkness. They obtained the sun and placed it in the sky to travel from east to west overhead every day. Initially, it was too hot, so they raised it multiple times until it reached a suitable position just under the celestial arch. The highest point is known as Gûlkwâ'gine Di'gălûñ'lătiyûñ' or "the seventh height," as it is seven hand-breadths above the Earth. The sun moves under this arch during the day and returns above it at night.

According to their belief, there is another world beneath ours, resembling ours in flora, fauna, and people, except for different seasons. The streams flowing from the mountains serve as paths to reach this underworld, and the springs at their source serve as gateways. However, to enter this realm, one must be quick and have a guide from the underground inhabitants. They know the seasons there differ from the outer world because the springs' water remains warmer in winter and cooler in summer than the surrounding air.

When animals and plants were created (the origin is unknown), they were commanded to stay awake and vigilant for seven nights, akin to how young people keep watch during their prayers to their medicine (spiritual guides). Many managed to stay awake during the first night, but sleep overcame them gradually, except for the owl, the panther, and a few others. These vigilant animals were granted the ability to see in the dark and to prey upon the birds and animals that sleep at night. Among the trees, only the cedar, pine, spruce, holly, and laurel successfully stayed awake, earning them the privilege of remaining evergreen and being highly regarded for medicinal properties. The other trees were told that they would lose their leaves every winter because they did not endure to the end of the vigil.

After animals and plants, humans were created. Initially, there were only a brother and sister until the brother struck the sister with a fish, instructing her to multiply. In just seven days, she gave birth to a child, and subsequently, every seven days, she bore another child, leading to an explosive increase in the population. To prevent overpopulation, it was decreed that women should only have one child per year, and this practice continues to this day.

The First Fire

In the beginning, there was no fire, and the world was cold until the Thunders (Ani'-Hyûñ'tĭkwălâ'skĭ), who resided in Gălûñ'lătĭ, decided to send their lightning to place fire into the hollow of a sycamore tree growing on an island. The animals knew about the fire's presence because they could see smoke rising from the tree's top, but the water surrounding the island made it inaccessible. Consequently, the animals held a council to determine what to do. This tale dates back to ancient times.

Every animal capable of flying or swimming was afraid to fetch the fire. The Raven volunteered first, being large and strong, and flew high and far across the water to the sycamore tree. However, he hesitated, and by the time he considered what to do, the intense heat had turned all his feathers black. Frightened, he returned without the fire. The little Screech-owl (Wa'huhu') offered to go next and reached the tree safely, but a blast of hot air from the hollow tree nearly burned out his eyes. He managed to fly back home, but his eyes remained red from the experience. Following this, the Hooting Owl (U'guku') and the Horned Owl (Tskĭlĭ') attempted the journey, but the fire had grown too fierce by the time they arrived, and the smoke almost blinded them, leaving white rings around their eyes. Despite their efforts, they couldn't remove these rings.

After the birds' unsuccessful attempts, the Uksu'hĭ snake, a black racer, bravely volunteered to swim across the water and bring back some fire. He crawled through the grass to the tree, entered through a small opening at the bottom, but the intense heat and smoke were too much for him. In his frantic escape, he ended up scorching his body black and ever since has had the habit of darting and doubling on his track as if trying to evade something. The great blacksnake, Gûle'gĭ, "The Climber," offered to go next. He swam to the island and climbed the tree's exterior as blacksnakes typically do. However, when he put his head into the hollow, the smoke overwhelmed him, and he fell into the burning stump, turning black just like the Uksu'hĭ snake.

With no success in obtaining fire yet, another council was held. Birds, snakes, and four-legged animals all had excuses for not going due to their fear of the burning sycamore. Eventually, Kănăne'skĭ Amai'yĕhĭ, the Water Spider, stepped forward. This is not the water spider that looks like a mosquito, but a different one with black downy hair and red stripes on her body. She could run on water or dive to the bottom, so reaching the island wasn't a problem. The concern was how she would bring back the fire. The resourceful Water Spider spun a thread from her body and wove it into a tusti bowl, fastening it to her back. She crossed over to the island, carefully gathered a small coal of fire into her bowl, and returned with it. Thanks to her efforts, humans have had fire ever since, and the Water Spider still retains her tusti bowl.

Kana'tĭ And Selu: The Inception Of Game And Corn

As a young boy, I listened to the elders recounting a tale from long ago. It was about a hunter named Kana'tĭ, and his wife Selu, who lived with their son at Pilot Knob. Kana'tĭ was known for always returning from the woods with a bountiful catch of game, which Selu would prepare by the river. One day, their son mentioned that he played with an unusual boy who emerged from the water, claiming to be his elder brother. This strange boy had come from the blood of the game washed off by Selu at the river.

The mysterious boy continued to play with Kana'tĭ's son daily, but always disappeared back into the water before anyone could see him. Kana'tĭ advised his son to wrestle with the boy and call for them when they had their arms around him. They did as instructed, and the boy struggled, revealing his true form as a wild and magical being named I'năge-utăsûñ'hĭ (He-who-grew-up-wild). They managed to capture him and bring him home, where they tried to tame him, but he remained wild and mischievous.

One day, the Wild Boy wanted to know where Kana'tĭ got all his game, so they followed him to a swamp, where he made arrows from reeds. The Wild Boy transformed into bird's down and landed on Kana'tĭ's shoulder, watching him make the arrows. They also discovered a place where Kana'tĭ kept the game animals and decided to release them all, except the bear which didn't exist then. This caused all the animals to scatter across the world.

They also learned the secret of Selu's abundant corn and beans supply. She magically produced them by rubbing her stomach and armpits. The boys suspected her of being a witch, so they killed her and followed her instructions to plant the corn. However, they neglected some steps, leading to the necessity of working the fields and tending the crop. The brothers later found their father, and together they journeyed to the end of the world.

They encountered dangers, but the boys proved themselves as great men with extraordinary abilities.

The Thunder Boys, as they were known, were later summoned by the people to bring back game using their magical songs. They performed seven compositions, summoning a herd of deer, and shared two of the songs with the hunters for future use. The Thunder Boys eventually returned to the Darkening land, and their songs have been preserved in the hunting tradition ever since.

Inception Of Diseases And Medicine

In ancient times, humans and all creatures lived harmoniously, and they could communicate with each other. However, as the human population grew rapidly and settlements expanded, the animals began to feel crowded and threatened. To make matters worse, humans invented weapons like bows, knives, and spears, leading to the hunting and killing of larger animals for food and their skins. Smaller creatures were often carelessly crushed or ignored.

The animals decided to hold councils to address the situation. The Bears were the first to convene, but they realized that imitating human weapons was not a viable solution. The Deer, on the other hand, decided to protect themselves by making hunters dream of snakes or consuming raw fish if they didn't ask for pardon after killing a deer. The Fishes and Reptiles also planned to influence humans' dreams, while the Birds, Insects, and smaller animals sought to inflict diseases as a form of retribution.

The Grubworm, pleased with the idea of diseases affecting humans, fell and twisted its body with joy. The plants, however, were sympathetic to humans and decided to counteract the diseases with their own remedies. They offered medicinal properties to counter the malevolent designs of the animals. Every plant agreed to help humans when called upon in times of need.

Thus, medicine was born, and the plants provided remedies for various diseases. Even weeds were created for a purpose, waiting for humans to discover their benefits. When a healer is unsure of which medicine to use, the spirit of the plant guides them.

The Daughter Of The Sun

On the opposite side of the firmament vault resided the Sun, while her daughter lived in the middle of the firmament, directly above the Earth. Each day, as the Sun journeyed westward along the firmament, she would pause at her daughter's house for dinner.

The Sun disliked the people on Earth because they could never look directly at her without squinting their faces. Complaining to her brother, the Moon, she mentioned that her grandchildren appeared unattractive as they grinned when they saw her. However, the Moon found them appealing, as they smiled warmly at him during his nightly appearance, thanks to his gentle rays.

Envious and bitter, the Sun devised a plan to kill all the people on Earth. When she reached her daughter's house, she would emit scorching rays, causing a deadly fever that claimed the lives of hundreds of people daily. Fearful of extinction, the people sought help from the Little Men, who advised them to kill the Sun to protect themselves.

The Little Men performed a powerful ritual, transforming two men into snakes, the Spreading-adder and the Copperhead, with the mission to bite the Sun. However, both attempts failed due to the Sun's radiant light, and the Copperhead accidentally bit the daughter, causing her death. With her daughter gone, the Sun withdrew, leaving the world in darkness.

To bring back the Sun's daughter and end the darkness, seven men were chosen for a quest to the Ghost country. Armed with sourwood rods and a box, they struck the daughter during a dance and trapped her in the box. On their journey home, she pleaded to be released but they obeyed the Little Men's instructions and kept the box closed. However, in a moment of weakness, they opened the box slightly, and she transformed into a redbird and flew away.

The Sun grieved for her lost daughter, and her tears threatened to flood the Earth. To comfort her, the people sent their best dancers and singers to entertain her. When the drummer altered the music, the Sun finally lifted her face, moved by the unexpected joy.

Thus, the redbird became known as the Sun's daughter, and the missed opportunity to bring her back from the Ghost country taught the people that once their loved ones pass on, they can never return. Despite the Sun's momentary happiness, the world remained dark without her daughter's radiant presence.

How They Brought Back The Tobacco

In the beginning of the world, when both people and animals were the same, there existed just one tobacco plant. They all used to gather there to obtain tobacco until the Dagûl'kû geese noticed it and carried it away to the south. Without tobacco, the people suffered, and there was an old woman who became frail and weak to the point where everyone believed she would soon die unless she could get some tobacco to sustain her.

Various animals offered to retrieve it, starting with the larger ones and then the smaller ones, but each time the Dagûl'kû would spot and kill them before they could reach the plant. Even the little Mole tried to reach it by going underground, but the Dagûl'kû detected his trail and killed him as he emerged.

Finally, the Hummingbird volunteered, but the others believed he was far too tiny and insisted he should stay home. He pleaded with them to let him try, so they showed him a plant in a field and asked him to demonstrate his approach. In an instant, the Hummingbird disappeared and reappeared sitting on the plant. He was so swift that nobody saw him coming or going. Confidently, he said, "This is how I'll do it," and they allowed him to proceed.

The Hummingbird flew eastward, and upon reaching the tobacco, he saw the Dagûl'kû guarding it. Yet, they couldn't spot him due to his small size and incredible speed. Swiftly, he darted down, snatched the top of the plant with its leaves and seeds, and flew away before the Dagûl'kû could react. By the time he returned home with the tobacco, the old woman had fainted, and they feared she was dead. But the Hummingbird blew the tobacco smoke into her nostrils, and with a cry of "Tsâ'lû! [Tobacco!]", she opened her eyes and came back to life.

SECOND VERSION

In the beginning, the people had tobacco, but they had used it all, leading to great suffering due to its scarcity. There was an elderly man so old that he relied on smoking to sustain himself, and his son, not wanting to see him perish, decided to venture southward and try to obtain more tobacco. The tobacco country was located far to the south, surrounded by tall mountains, and guarded passages, making it extremely challenging to access. However, the young man was a skilled conjurer and had no fear. He journeyed south until he reached the mountains bordering the tobacco country. There, he opened his medicine bag, took out a hummingbird skin, and draped it over himself like a garment. Transformed into a hummingbird, he effortlessly flew over the mountains to the tobacco fields. Gathering some leaves and seeds, he stored them in his medicine bag. His small and swift form made him invisible to the sentinels, and he was able to carry as much as he needed. Returning in the same manner, he removed the hummingbird skin, becoming a man again. He began his journey back home. During his travels, he came across a tree with an opening in its trunk, resembling a doorway, and a magnificent woman peering out from it. Intrigued, he tried to climb the tree, but despite being a skilled climber, he kept slipping back. However, when he put on a pair of magical moccasins from his pouch, he could climb the tree with ease. Yet, every time he looked up, the opening seemed to be even further away. Exhausted, he descended the tree and returned home. There, he found his father frail but still alive. One puff from the pipe revitalized him. The people then planted the seeds the young man brought back, and they have had tobacco ever since.

The Peregrination To The Sunrise

Many years ago, a group of young men made a firm decision to seek out the dwelling place of the Sun and discover what the Sun resembled. Fully prepared with their bows, arrows, dried corn, and extra moccasins, they set out on their journey toward the east. Initially, they encountered tribes they were familiar with, then encountered ones they had only heard about, and finally came across tribes they had never even heard a whisper of.

Among the tribes they encountered were root eaters and acorn eaters, with large piles of acorn shells near their homes. In one tribe, they found a sick man on the verge of death. They learned that it was their custom to bury a man's wife in the same grave with him upon his demise. The young men waited until the man passed away, and they witnessed his friends lowering his body into a deep and dark pit, its bottom hidden from view. Then, they observed a rope being tied around the woman's body, along with a bundle of pine knots. A lit pine knot was placed in her hand, and she was lowered into the pit to meet her end in the darkness after the last pine knot burned out.

The journey continued until they finally arrived at the place where the Sun rises, where the sky meets the ground. There, they discovered that the sky was an arched vault of solid rock suspended above the earth, perpetually swinging up and down. As it went up, a doorway-like opening appeared between the sky and the ground, and when it swung back, the door closed shut. The Sun emerged from this door in the east and traversed along the inner side of the arch. Although the Sun had a human figure, its brilliance prevented them from clearly discerning its form, and its intense heat kept them from approaching too closely. They waited until the Sun had risen and attempted to pass through the doorway while it was still open. However, as the first young man was in the doorway, the rock descended and crushed him. The remaining six were too afraid to attempt the feat. Now at the edge of the world, they turned back and began their journey homeward.

However, the long travels had taken their toll, and by the time they returned home, they had become old men.

The Moon And The Thunders

Long ago, the Sun was a young woman residing in the East, while her brother, the Moon, lived in the West. The Sun had an admirer who would come every month during the dark phase of the Moon to court her. They would meet at night, and before daylight, he would depart. In the darkness, she could not see his face, and he would not reveal his identity, leaving her wondering about his true nature. To find out who he was, she devised a plan. The next time they met in the dark of the night, she discreetly dipped her hand into the cinders and ashes of the fireplace and gently rubbed it over his face, pretending to sympathize with him for having a cold face due to the wind. Unaware of the ashes on her hand, he left after some time.

When the Moon rose into the sky the following night, his face was covered with spots, and the Sun realized he was the one who had been courting her. He was embarrassed by her discovery and tried to keep as far away from her as possible on the other side of the sky throughout the night. Since then, he has attempted to maintain a considerable distance from the Sun, and when he does come close to her in the west, he appears thin as a ribbon, barely visible.

According to some elders, the moon is said to be a ball that was thrown up against the sky in a game long ago. In a match between two towns, one team nearly won, but the opposing team's leader used his hand (which was against the rules) to throw the ball towards the goal. However, the ball struck the solid sky vault and became lodged there as a reminder never to cheat. When the moon appears small and pale, it is believed that someone has mishandled the ball. Thus, in the past, games were only played during a full moon.

During an eclipse of the sun or moon, it is believed that a giant frog in the sky is trying to swallow it. To counter this, people used to gather and create loud noises like firing guns and beating drums to scare off the frog and restore the sun or moon to its normal state.

The Sun and Moon are commonly referred to as Nûñdă, with one being "Nûñdă that dwells in the day" and the other "Nûñdă that dwells in the night." However, the priests have different names for them, calling the Sun "Su'tălidihĭ'," which means "Six-killer," and the Moon "Ge''yăgu'ga," though the meanings of these names have been forgotten. Some people ask the Moon not to bring rain or snow.

Above the sky vault, the great Thunder and his two sons, known as the Thunder boys, reside in the far west. Lightning and the rainbow represent their majestic appearance. The priests pray to the Thunder, calling him the Red Man due to the brilliant color of his attire. Other Thunders live lower down, within cliffs, mountains, and under waterfalls, traveling on invisible bridges between high peaks where they have their dwellings. The great Thunders above the sky are benevolent and helpful when prayed to, but the others are mischievous and may cause harm. One must be careful not to point at the rainbow, as it is believed to cause swelling in the finger's lower joint.

What The Stars Are Like

Opinions about the stars vary among people. Some believe they are balls of light, while others think they have a human form. However, the majority describe them as living creatures covered in radiant fur or feathers.

During one night, a hunting party camping in the mountains noticed two bright lights resembling huge stars moving along the top of a distant ridge. Intrigued, they observed the lights until they disappeared on the other side. The following nights, the lights reappeared, moving along the ridge. After discussing the matter, they decided to investigate the cause and planned to do so the next day. When morning came, they set out and eventually reached the ridge. After searching for some time, they discovered two peculiar creatures, about as large as one could make a circle with outstretched arms. These creatures had round bodies covered in fine fur or downy feathers, with small heads resembling terrapins sticking out. When the wind blew, sparks would fly out from their feathers.

Curious, the hunters brought these peculiar beings back to their camp, intending to take them to their settlements upon their return. For several days, they observed that every night, these creatures would glow and shine brightly like great stars. In the day, they appeared as mere gray fur balls, except when the wind stirred and the sparks flew out. The creatures remained silent, and no one suspected they would attempt to escape. However, on the seventh night, they suddenly ascended from the ground, turning into balls of fire, and swiftly soared above the treetops. Higher and higher they went, mesmerizing the watching hunters, until they transformed into two brilliant points of light in the dark sky, revealing their true identity as stars.

Inchoation Of The Pleiades And The Pine

In the distant past, during the early days of the world's existence, there were seven boys who would spend all their time near the townhouse playing a game called gatayû'stĭ. This game involves rolling a stone wheel on the ground and using a curved stick to strike it. Despite their mothers' scolding, the boys remained engrossed in the game. One day, in an attempt to teach them a lesson, their mothers boiled some gatayû'stĭ stones along with the corn for dinner. When the hungry boys returned home, their mothers served them the stones, saying, "Since you seem to prefer gatayû'stĭ over the cornfield, you can have these stones for your dinner."

The boys were furious and decided to go down to the townhouse, saying, "Since our mothers treat us this way, let's go somewhere we won't trouble them anymore." They initiated a dance, some believe it was the Feather dance, and circled the townhouse, praying to the spirits for assistance. Unaware of what was happening, their mothers grew worried and went out to look for them. To their astonishment, they saw the boys still dancing around the townhouse, but with each round, the boys were rising higher and higher into the air. The mothers rushed to reach their children, but it was too late; all but one had ascended above the roof of the townhouse. One of the mothers managed to pull her son down using the gatayû'stĭ stick, but he struck the ground so hard that he disappeared into it, and the earth closed over him.

The remaining six boys continued to circle higher and higher until they reached the sky. Today, we know them as the Pleiades, referred to by the Cherokee people as Ani'tsutsă (The Boys). The community mourned the loss of the boys, but the mother whose son had gone into the ground visited the spot every morning and evening, grieving until the earth was moist with her tears. Eventually, a small green shoot sprouted and grew day by day, becoming the tall pine tree we know today. The pine tree possesses the same radiant light as the stars in the sky, connecting it to the fate of the lost boys.

The Milky Way

In the southern region, there were some people who owned a corn mill used to pound corn into a meal. Several mornings, they noticed that some of the meal had been stolen during the night. Upon inspecting the ground, they discovered canine tracks. Determined to catch the culprit, they decided to keep watch the following night. As the canine emerged from the north and began eating from the bowl of meal, they surprised him and gave him a whipping. The canine howled and hurried back to his home in the north, dropping the stolen meal from his mouth as he ran. His path left a white trail in the sky, which we now know as the Milky Way. The Cherokee people still refer to it as Gi'lĭ'-utsûñ'stănûñ'yĭ, meaning "Where the canine ran."

Inchoation Of Strawberries

After the first man was created and given a mate, they lived together happily for a while. However, their blissful existence took a turn when they started quarreling. Eventually, the woman decided to leave her husband and journeyed towards Nûñdâgûñ'yĭ, the land of the Sun, in the east. The man, feeling lonely and sorrowful, followed her, hoping to reconcile.

As the woman continued on her path without looking back, Une''lănûñ'hĭ, the great Apportioner (the Sun), took pity on the man. Une''lănûñ'hĭ asked the man if he was still angry with his wife, and he replied that he was not. Then, Une''lănûñ'hĭ inquired if the man would like to have his wife back, and he enthusiastically said yes.

To facilitate their reunion, Une''lănûñ'hĭ caused a patch of the finest ripe huckleberries to grow along the woman's path. However, she paid no attention to them. Further along, he placed a clump of blackberries, which she also ignored. Despite placing various tempting fruits and beautiful red accommodation berries near her path, she pressed on.

Finally, she came across an extraordinary patch of ripe strawberries, the likes of which had never been seen before. As she picked some to eat, she happened to glance towards the west, triggering memories of her husband to flood back into her mind. Overwhelmed with longing, she found herself unable to continue her journey. Sitting down, her desire to be with her husband grew stronger with each passing moment. Eventually, she gathered a bunch of the finest berries and turned back along the path to offer them to her husband.

When they met again, they embraced each other warmly and decided to return home together, reuniting in love and harmony once more.

The Great Yellow-Jacket: Inchoation Of Fish And Frogs

In ancient times, the inhabitants of Kanu'ga'lâ'yĭ, also known as Briertown, located along the Nantahala River in present-day Macon County, North Carolina, were greatly troubled by a massive insect named U'la'gû'. This insect was as huge as a house and would suddenly appear from its hidden lair, swiftly snatching children away while they played. It was a unique and unknown creature, and the people attempted numerous times to trace its origin but failed due to its incredible speed.

In their pursuit to understand and capture the U'la'gû', they devised a plan. They tied a white string to a squirrel they killed, hoping to follow its course with their eyes, much like bee hunters track the flight of bees to find their hive. When the U'la'gû' came, it carried away the squirrel with the attached string, but it moved so swiftly through the air that it disappeared from sight in an instant. Undeterred, they tried again with a turkey and then a deer ham, using longer strings each time, but the creature remained too elusive to be tracked.

Finally, they killed a young deer and attached an exceptionally long white string to it. When the U'la'gû' returned, it seized the deer, but the load was so heavy that it had to fly slowly and at a lower height, making the string visible to the hunters.

Determined to confront the creature, the hunters followed its flight path eastward, eventually arriving near the present-day location of Franklin. Across the valley, they spotted the U'la'gû''s nest within a large cave in the rocks. Ecstatic, they shouted and hurriedly made their way down the mountain and across to the cave.

The nest had an entrance below, with multiple cells built up one above another to the cave's roof. Inside, they found the gigantic U'la'gû' and numerous smaller creatures now known as yellow-jackets. To deal with the threat, the hunters built fires around the cave's entrance, filling it with smoke. This suffocated the giant insect and many of the smaller ones inside the cave. However, some yellow-jackets managed to escape and multiply, leading to their presence throughout the world today.

The cave was henceforth called Tsgâgûñ'yĭ, meaning "Where the yellow-jacket was," while the place from which they first spotted the nest was named A'tahi'ta, signifying "Where they shouted," and these names still endure.

According to their stories, all fish and frogs were believed to originate from a colossal monster fish and frog that caused significant damage. Eventually, the people killed these creatures and cut them into pieces, which were then thrown into the water. These fragments took on the form of smaller fish and frogs, populating the waters thereafter.

The Deluge

In ancient times, there lived a man who had a dog that would go to the river daily to examine the water and howl. Growing annoyed, the man scolded the dog, who then spoke to him, saying, "Very soon, there will be a tremendous flood, and the water will rise so high that everyone will drown. But if you build a raft before the rain comes, you can save yourself. However, you must first throw me into the water." Skeptical, the man doubted the dog's words. To prove its sincerity, the dog told the man to check the back of its neck, where the skin was worn off, revealing the bones.

Convinced of the impending disaster, the man began constructing a raft. When the rain arrived, he gathered his family and ample provisions, and they all boarded the raft. The rain poured incessantly, causing the water to rise until it covered the mountains, and everyone in the world drowned. As the rain finally stopped and the waters receded, it became safe to leave the raft. Only the man and his family remained alive.

One day, they heard sounds of dancing and shouting from the other side of the ridge. Curious, the man climbed to the top to look over and saw a still landscape, but along the valley were immense piles of bones from the drowned people. Realizing that the ghosts of the deceased had been engaged in a spectral dance.

The Four Footed Tribes

In Cherokee mythology, there is no fundamental distinction between humans and animals. During the primordial times, all creatures coexisted harmoniously, living and working together until humans' aggression and disregard for others' rights led to conflict. Insects, birds, fish, reptiles, and four-legged beasts united against humans, creating a separation between their lives. However, this distinction is only a matter of degree, as both humans and animals are organized into tribes with chiefs, townhouses, councils, and ballplays. In the afterlife, they believe in a Darkening land called Usûñhi'yǐ.

Despite man's dominant position, he must appease the animal tribes whenever he hunts and slaughters them. The concept of reincarnation plays a role here, as every animal is believed to have a specific life term. If killed before the allotted time, the animal temporarily dies and is immediately resurrected in its original form. This belief is supported by myths like the bear man and the tale of the Little Deer.

Certain supernatural figures like Kana'tǐ and Tsul'kǎlû' have control over the animals and are considered the deities of the hunters. They play significant roles in Cherokee folklore.

Various animals hold special meaning and symbolism for the Cherokee. The Rabbit is seen as a trickster, the Bat is revered for its dodging abilities, and the Deer has important roles in myths and ceremonies. The Bear has its own chief and townhouses, while the Wolf is considered the watchdog of Kana'tǐ.

Other animals like the Canine, Elephant, Fox, Skunk, and Beaver also appear in Cherokee beliefs and practices, each with its unique characteristics and associations.

Throughout these myths and folklore, the Cherokee's deep connection with nature and the animal kingdom is evident, reflecting their reverence and understanding of the world around them.

The Rabbit Goes Duck Hunting

The Rabbit was excessively boastful, often claiming that he could do anything he saw others do. He was so cunning that he could easily deceive the other animals with his tricks. Once, he pretended that he could swim and catch fish just like the Otter. The other animals challenged him to prove it, and he set up a clever plan that led to the Otter's embarrassment.

Later on, when they met again, the Otter mentioned that he sometimes ate ducks. The Rabbit promptly replied that he did the same. The Otter dared him to try it, and they approached a group of ducks in the river without being noticed. The Otter fearlessly dove into the water, swimming underneath until he caught a duck without being seen. The Rabbit, however, had a trick up his sleeve. He had prepared a noose from bark and dived into the water. Struggling to hold his breath, he swam closer to the ducks and managed to catch one with the noose. He held on tightly, but the duck flew into the air, pulling the Rabbit along until he lost his grip.

The Rabbit fell into a tall, hollow sycamore stump with no way out. Hungry and weak, he remained trapped for days until he could hardly bear it. When he heard children playing outside, he sang a song to get their attention. The children ran to tell their father, who came to cut a hole in the tree. The Rabbit kept singing, encouraging them to make the hole larger so they could see his beauty. When they stepped back to get a good look, the clever Rabbit seized his chance, jumped out, and escaped before they could catch him.

How The Rabbit Purloined The Otter's Coat

The animals varied in size, donning coats of different colors and patterns. Some sported long fur while others had shorter fur. Tails were present in some, adorned with rings, while others had no tails at all. Their relentless debates about their appearances led to a unanimous decision to hold a council and settle once and for all who possessed the most magnificent coat among them.

The Otter, a creature living far up the creek and rarely seen by the others, was reputed to have the most splendid coat. However, as no one had laid eyes on him for quite some time, they were uncertain about the specifics of his appearance. Though they only knew the general direction of his dwelling, they were confident he would attend the council once they spread the word.

The Rabbit, yearning for the title, plotted to deceive the Otter and claim the accolade for himself. With crafty inquiries, the Rabbit learned the route the Otter would take to reach the council grounds. Without revealing his intentions, the Rabbit set out ahead of the Otter and after four days' travel, he encountered the Otter. The Rabbit recognized him immediately by his lustrous coat of soft, dark-brown fur. Delighted to see the Rabbit, the Otter inquired about his journey. The Rabbit responded, saying that the other animals had sent him to accompany the Otter since he lived so far away, and they were worried he might not know the way. The Otter thanked the Rabbit, and together they continued towards the council.

Throughout the day, they journeyed towards the council site, and as evening approached, the Rabbit picked a suitable campsite for the Otter, who was unfamiliar with the area. He arranged comfortable beds with bushes and ensured everything was well-prepared. The next morning, they resumed their journey, and in the afternoon, the Rabbit collected wood and bark, carrying them on his back. When asked by the curious Otter about the purpose of this, the Rabbit explained that it was to keep them warm and comfortable during the night.

As sunset neared, they settled down to make camp. The Rabbit then fashioned a paddle from a stick, claiming that he had good dreams when sleeping with a paddle under his head. This intrigued the Otter, who inquired about its use. The Rabbit then revealed that they were in a place called "Di'tatlâski'yĭ" or "The Place Where it Rains Fire." He devised a plan to deceive the Otter by making him believe it could rain fire in that area.

The Rabbit suggested the Otter sleep while he stayed awake to keep watch. He told the Otter to run and jump into the river if he spotted any signs of fire. The Otter followed the Rabbit's instructions and went to sleep, leaving his coat hanging on a limb nearby.

As night fell, the Rabbit called out, pretending that it was raining fire. The Otter, still half-asleep, didn't respond immediately. The Rabbit tried again, this time filling the paddle with hot coals and throwing them into the air, shouting, "It's raining fire! It's raining fire!"

Alarmed, the Otter jumped up, and the Rabbit urged him to run to the water. The Otter ran and leaped into the river, where he has lived ever since.

With the Otter gone, the Rabbit swapped his own coat with the Otter's resplendent fur and continued to the council. The other animals eagerly awaited the Otter's arrival. When they finally spotted him in the distance, they excitedly informed each other, and one of the smaller animals was sent to show him the best seat. As they approached him to welcome him, they were perplexed by his bashful demeanor, covering his face with a paw.

The Bear, intrigued by the Otter's behavior, removed the paw, revealing the Rabbit's split nasal discerner. Realizing the deception, the Rabbit swiftly fled, but the Bear managed to snatch his tail, leaving the Rabbit tailless from that day onward.

Why The Possum's Tail Is Bare

The Possum was once blessed with a long, bushy tail that filled him with immense pride. Every morning, he would diligently groom it and boast about it during the dances. However, the Rabbit, who had lost his own tail when the Bear yanked it out, grew incredibly envious. Determined to play a trick on the Possum, the Rabbit devised a cunning plan.

A grand council and dance were scheduled, where all the animals were expected to attend. It was the Rabbit's responsibility to spread the news, so as he passed by the Possum's dwelling, he stopped to inquire if the Possum intended to join. The Possum expressed his willingness to come but requested a special seat, stating, "Because I have such a handsome tail, I ought to sit where everyone can see me." The Rabbit assured the Possum that he would take care of it and promised to send someone to groom and dress the Possum's tail for the dance. Delighted, the Possum agreed to attend.

The Rabbit then approached the Cricket, known for his exceptional hair-cutting skills, and instructed him to visit the Possum's home the next morning and groom his tail for the dance that night. The Rabbit provided detailed instructions to the Cricket and then went about causing mischief elsewhere.

The next morning, the Cricket arrived at the Possum's house, informing him that he had come to prepare him for the dance. The Possum stretched out and closed his eyes while the Cricket combed his tail and wrapped a red string around it to keep it smooth until the dance. Unbeknownst to the Possum, the Cricket was secretly snipping off the hair near the roots while winding the string.

As night fell, the Possum arrived at the townhouse for the dance and found the promised best seat waiting for him, just as the Rabbit had pledged. When it was his turn to dance, he untied the string from his tail and stepped into the center of the floor. The drummers began to play, and the Possum proudly sang, "See my beautiful tail." The crowd cheered, and he danced around the circle, singing again, "See what a fine color it has." The cheers grew louder, and he danced around once more, singing, "See how it sweeps the ground." The animals cheered more enthusiastically than ever, and the Possum felt delighted. He danced around again and sang, "See how fine the fur is." At that moment, everyone burst into laughter, and the Possum couldn't understand why. As he looked around the circle of animals, he saw them all laughing at him. He then glanced down at his once magnificent tail and realized that not a single hair remained; it was as bare as a lizard's tail. He was so astonished and embarrassed that he couldn't utter a word. Helplessly, he rolled on the ground and grinned, just as the Possum does to this day when taken by surprise.

How The Wildcat Caught The Gobbler

Once, the Wildcat managed to capture the Rabbit, and it seemed like the end for the poor Rabbit. However, the clever Rabbit pleaded for his life, saying, "I am so small that I would barely satisfy your hunger, but if you spare me, I will show you where you can find a whole flock of Turkeys." Intrigued by the prospect, the Wildcat released the Rabbit and agreed to follow him to the Turkeys' location.

As they approached the Turkeys, the Rabbit instructed the Wildcat, "You must do exactly as I say. Pretend to be dead and remain motionless, even if I kick you. But when I give the signal, jump up and catch the largest Turkey you see." The Wildcat agreed and lay down, pretending to be dead. Meanwhile, the Rabbit gathered some rotten wood and rubbed it over the Wildcat's eyes and nose to make them appear flyblown, convincing the Turkeys that he had been dead for a while.

The Rabbit then went to the Turkeys and spoke in a friendly manner, "Look, I found our old enemy, the Wildcat, lying dead on the path. Let's have a dance over him." Although the Turkeys were skeptical, they followed the Rabbit to where the Wildcat lay motionless on the road. The Rabbit had a wonderful singing voice and was a skilled dance leader. He said, "I will lead the music, and you can dance around him." The Turkeys agreed, and the Rabbit used a stick to beat time while singing, "Gălăgi'na hasuyak', Gălăgi'na hasuyak'" (pick out the Gobbler, pick out the Gobbler).

"Why do you say that?" asked the old Turkey. "Oh, don't worry," replied the Rabbit, "that's just how we do it, and we sing this way." He began the song again, and the Turkeys danced around the supposedly lifeless Wildcat. After several rounds, the Rabbit said, "Now, go and hit him, just like we do in the war dance." Believing the Wildcat to be truly dead, the Turkeys crowded around him, and the old gobbler gave him a kick. At that moment, the Rabbit drummed vigorously and sang loudly, "Pick out the Gobbler,

pick out the Gobbler," and the Wildcat swiftly jumped up and caught the Gobbler.

How The Terrapin Beat The Rabbit

The Rabbit was widely renowned for his incredible speed, and this fact was well-known to everyone. On the other hand, the Terrapin was considered a slow walker, but he took great pride in his prowess as a warrior and often engaged in disputes with the Rabbit about their respective swiftness. Finally, they agreed to settle the matter through a race. They set the day, the starting point, and decided to run across four mountain ridges, with the first one to reach the finish line being declared the winner.

Confident in his abilities, the Rabbit taunted the Terrapin, saying, "You know you can't run. You'll never win this race, so I'll give you a head start by letting you cross the first ridge while I'll have four ridges to conquer."

The Terrapin agreed to this arrangement but, that night, he secretly summoned his Terrapin friends and sought their assistance. He admitted that he couldn't outrun the Rabbit, but he was determined to put an end to the Rabbit's boasting. He shared his plan with his friends, and they agreed to help him.

On the race day, all the animals gathered to witness the event. The Rabbit joined the crowd, but the Terrapin had already gone ahead toward the first ridge as they had planned, and he was cleverly hidden among the tall grass. The race began, and the Rabbit started with long leaps up the mountain, expecting to reach the finish line before the Terrapin could even descend the other side. However, to his surprise, when he reached the top of the first ridge, he saw the Terrapin already crossing over.

The Rabbit continued on, but each time he reached a ridge, the Terrapin was already ahead of him. Despite his desperate efforts, the Rabbit couldn't catch up. Exhausted and out of breath, he finally reached the top of the fourth ridge just in time to witness the Terrapin triumphantly crossing the finish line.

The Rabbit couldn't take another leap and collapsed on the ground, making distressed sounds, "mĭ, mĭ, mĭ, mĭ," as the Rabbit does ever since when he is too weary to run any further. The Terrapin was declared the winner, leaving all the animals astonished at how he could outsmart the Rabbit. However, the Terrapin kept his strategy a secret, and no one knew how he managed to defeat the Rabbit.

In present times, during preparations for the ball game, the conjurer cooks plenty of rabbit hamstrings into a soup and pours it across the path where the other players will walk the next morning. The idea is to make them tired in a similar manner so that they may lose the game. However, this tactic is not always successful, as the opposing team might be aware of it and have watchers ahead to prevent its impact.

The Rabbit And The Tar Wolf

During a prolonged period of dry weather, the creeks and springs ran dry, prompting the animals to convene a council to find a solution. They collectively decided to dig a well, and all agreed to help, except for the Rabbit, who was known for being lazy and said, "I don't need to dig for water. The dew on the grass is enough for me." The others were displeased with his response, but they proceeded to work together and dug the well.

They noticed that, despite the ongoing dry weather and the decreasing water level in the well, the Rabbit remained well-fed and lively. Suspecting that the sly Rabbit was stealing their water at night, they decided to craft a wolf figure using pine gum and tar. They positioned the dummy next to the well to scare off the thief. That night, as usual, the Rabbit came to drink and saw the peculiar black figure by the well. He asked, "Who's there?" but the tar wolf remained silent. With growing confidence, the Rabbit approached closer and threatened, "Move out of my way, or I'll strike you." Yet, the wolf statue remained motionless, emboldening the Rabbit to strike it with his paw. However, the sticky gum held his foot fast, trapping him on the spot.

Now infuriated, the Rabbit threatened again, "Release me, or I'll kick you!" Still, the wolf made no response. In his frustration, the Rabbit struck again with his hind foot, but this time, it too became ensnared in the gum, leaving him unable to move. The Rabbit remained stuck until the other animals came to fetch water in the morning. Discovering the identity of the thief, they initially had some fun teasing him before planning to put an end to his mischief. However, as soon as the Rabbit was freed from the tar wolf, he managed to escape before they could take any action against him.

SECOND VERSION

"Once in a land afflicted by a harsh and unyielding drought, all the streams and lakes ran dry. In this desperate situation, the animals gathered together to devise a plan to procure water. One suggestion was to dig a well, and all the animals, except for the hare, agreed to contribute to the effort. The hare hesitated, concerned that her delicate paws would get dirty in the process. Despite her reluctance, the other animals dug the well and were fortunate enough to find water.

As time passed, the hare started to suffer from thirst and had no access to the well. Left to her own devices, she resorted to stealing water from the public well as the easiest solution. The other animals were astonished to see her well-supplied with water and asked her where she got it. She claimed that she collected dewdrops by waking up early in the morning. However, the wolf and the fox, suspicious of her explanations, devised a plan to catch her in the act.

They crafted a wolf figure out of tar and placed it near the well. On the following night, when the hare came as usual to get her water, she noticed the tar wolf and demanded to know who was there. Receiving no response, she issued the command again, threatening to kick the wolf if it remained silent. Still, there was no answer, and when she attempted to kick the wolf, her paw got stuck in the tar, and she was caught.

The fox and the wolf then deliberated on what to do with her. One suggested beheading her, but the hare protested, claiming it had been attempted before without harm. Other methods were proposed to dispatch her, but she dismissed them as futile. Finally, they decided to release her to perish in a thicket. The hare acted distressed and pleaded for her life, but her enemies paid little attention and set her free.

As soon as she was out of their reach, the hare let out a triumphant cry and bounded away, declaring, 'This is where I live!'"

The Rabbit And The Possum After a Wife

Both the Rabbit and the Possum desired to find wives, but they were unsuccessful in their endeavors. They discussed their situation, and the Rabbit came up with a plan. He proposed traveling to the next settlement, where he, as the council's herald, would declare an important order that everyone must marry immediately. This way, they believed they would surely find their desired partners.

Enthusiastic about the idea, they set off together towards the next town. The Rabbit, being faster, reached the settlement first and waited outside until he was noticed and invited into the townhouse. Upon meeting the chief, the Rabbit delivered the council's message, and as a result, all the animals in the town promptly found their mates, and the Rabbit got himself a wife.

Meanwhile, the Possum's slow pace caused him to arrive after all the animals had already paired up, leaving him still without a spouse. The Rabbit pretended to sympathize with his friend and offered to carry the message to the next settlement. He advised the Possum to hurry as fast as he could, assuring him that this time he would undoubtedly find a wife.

However, when the Rabbit reached the next town, he cleverly spread false information. He proclaimed that the council had mandated an immediate war, and the fighting should commence right there in the townhouse. Chaos ensued as the animals started battling one another. The Rabbit, using his agility, managed to escape while the Possum arrived just in time to witness the mayhem. Unaware of the deception, the Possum found himself under attack, defenseless without his weapons, and was nearly beaten to death. He cunningly pretended to be lifeless until he saw an opportunity to escape. From that day on, the Possum learned a lesson. Whenever cornered by hunters, he would shut his eyes and feign death to evade capture.

The Rabbit Dines The Bear

The Bear extended an invitation to the Rabbit for a dinner together. They planned to cook beans, but lacked the necessary grease. In a resourceful move, the Bear made a slit in his side, allowing the oil to flow out until they had enough for their meal. The Rabbit was intrigued and thought, "That's a clever idea. I think I'll try it too." As he headed back home, he invited the Bear to join him for dinner after four days.

When the appointed day arrived, the Bear went to the Rabbit's home. The Rabbit cheerfully exclaimed, "I have beans for dinner, and something extra. I'll fetch the grease for cooking now." With a knife in hand, he attempted to replicate the Bear's technique by cutting into his side. However, instead of oil, a torrent of blood gushed out, and the Rabbit collapsed, near death. The Bear hurriedly attended to him, binding the wound to stop the bleeding. Angrily, he scolded the Rabbit, "You foolish little creature! I am large, strong, and well-covered with fat all over; the knife does me no harm. But you are small and lean, and you can't attempt such feats."

The Rabbit Eludes From The Wolves

Once, some Wolves managed to capture the Rabbit and were planning to devour him. However, the clever Rabbit devised a cunning plan. He requested their permission to demonstrate a new dance he had been practicing. Knowing that the Rabbit was an excellent dance leader, and eager to learn the latest dance, the Wolves agreed and formed a circle around him as he prepared to perform.

The Rabbit began to pat his feet and gracefully danced in a circular pattern, singing a lively tune:

"Tlâge'situñ' găli'sgi'sidâ'hă—
Ha'nia lĭl! lĭl! Ha'nia lĭl! lĭl!
On the edge of the field I dance about—
Ha'nia lĭl! lĭl! Ha'nia lĭl! lĭl!"

He then explained to the Wolves that when he sang "on the edge of the field," he would dance in that direction, and when he sang "lĭl! lĭl!" they were to stamp their feet vigorously. The Wolves were delighted and eagerly followed his instructions.

With each round, the Rabbit sang louder and danced closer to the field. As the Wolves were completely engrossed in the dance, he seized the opportunity. On the fourth round, while the Wolves were energetically stamping their feet to the beat of the song, the Rabbit made a swift leap and dashed off through the tall grass.

The Wolves quickly pursued him, but the Rabbit was cunning. He ran to a hollow stump and nimbly climbed up inside. When the Wolves arrived at the stump, one of them attempted to peer inside, but the Rabbit spat into his eye, forcing him to withdraw in discomfort. The other Wolves were too afraid to attempt it themselves, and so they reluctantly departed, leaving the Rabbit safely hidden within the stump.

Flint Visits The Rabbit

In ancient times, Tăwi'skălă (Flint) resided in the mountains, and the animals dreaded him due to his prowess in hunting and killing many of them. They convened to discuss ways to get rid of him, but no one dared to approach his abode until the bold Rabbit offered to confront Flint and attempt to eliminate him. They revealed Flint's location to the Rabbit, and he set out on his quest, finally arriving at Flint's dwelling.

Flint was standing at the entrance when the Rabbit approached and jeered, "Siyu'! Hello! Are you the one they call Flint?" Flint confirmed his identity, and the Rabbit continued to survey the area, seeking a way to catch Flint off guard. Expecting an invitation inside, the Rabbit hesitated, but as Flint showed no sign of hospitality, the Rabbit suggested, "Well, I am Rabbit; I've heard much about you, so I came to invite you to visit me."

Flint was curious about the location of the Rabbit's dwelling, and the Rabbit told him it was in the broom-grass field near the river. Flint agreed to visit in a few days. The Rabbit persisted, "Why not come now and share supper with me?" After some coaxing, Flint consented, and the two started down the mountain together.

Approaching the Rabbit's den, the Rabbit remarked, "This is my house, but during summer, I prefer staying outside where it's cooler." They had supper on the grass, and after the meal, Flint laid down to rest. Seizing the opportunity, the Rabbit fetched hefty sticks and his knife, crafting a mallet and wedge. Flint inquired about the tools, and the Rabbit casually replied that he enjoyed being occupied, and they might be useful. Flint dozed off again, and when he appeared sound asleep, the Rabbit made his move.

With one forceful blow, the Rabbit drove the sharp stake into Flint's body and raced back to his own den. However, just before reaching safety, there was a loud explosion, and flint fragments scattered everywhere, explaining why flint can now be found in various places. One piece struck the Rabbit from behind, cutting him just as he dived into his den. He *cautiously waited until all was quiet, then peeked outside, but another falling piece hit him on the lip, leaving a permanent split. That is the reason for the Rabbit's distinctive appearance to this day.*

How The Deer Got His Horns

In the beginning, the Deer didn't have horns; his head was smooth, resembling a doe's. He was a remarkable runner, and the Rabbit was an excellent jumper. The other animals were curious to determine who could go farther simultaneously. After much discussion, they organized a competition between the two and prepared a beautiful, large pair of antlers as the prize for the winner. The race would begin at one side of a thicket, go through it, then turn around and return, and the first one to emerge from the other side would receive the antlers.

On the appointed day, all the animals gathered, and the antlers were placed on the ground at the thicket's edge to mark the starting point. While everyone admired the prize, the Rabbit said, "I'm not familiar with this part of the area; I'd like to take a look through the bushes where I'll be running." They agreed, and the Rabbit entered the thicket. However, he took so long that the animals began to suspect he might be up to one of his tricks. They sent a messenger to search for him, and deep inside the thicket, the messenger found the Rabbit, cutting down the bushes and clearing a path almost to the other side.

The messenger silently returned and informed the other animals. When the Rabbit finally emerged, they accused him of cheating, but he denied it until they entered the thicket and discovered the cleared path. Convinced that such a cunning trickster shouldn't be allowed in the race, they awarded the antlers to the Deer, acknowledging him as the superior runner, and he has worn them ever since. They told the Rabbit that since he enjoyed cutting down bushes so much, he should make a living doing that from then on, and he has been doing so ever since.

Why The Deer's Teeth Are Blunt

The Rabbit was feeling resentful because the Deer had won the antlers (refer to the previous story), and he was determined to get revenge. One day, shortly after the race, he placed a large grapevine across the trail and gnawed it almost in two at the center. Then he went back a distance, took a running start, and leaped up at the vine. He kept running and jumping at the vine repeatedly until the Deer approached and asked him what he was doing.

"Don't you see?" said the Rabbit. "I'm so strong that I can bite through that grapevine in one jump."

The Deer found this hard to believe and wanted to witness it for himself. So the Rabbit ran back, made an impressive leap, and bit through the vine where he had gnawed it before. The Deer, upon seeing this, said, "Well, if you can do it, I can too." The Rabbit then stretched out a larger grapevine across the trail but didn't gnaw it in the middle.

The Deer imitated the Rabbit, running back and making a spring, but when he struck the vine in the center, it simply flew back and threw him over on his head. He tried again and again, becoming bruised and bleeding in the process.

"Let me see your teeth," finally said the Rabbit. The Deer showed him his teeth, which were long but not very sharp, resembling a wolf's teeth.

"No wonder you can't do it," said the Rabbit. "Your teeth are too blunt. Let me sharpen them like mine. My teeth are so sharp that I can cut through a stick like a knife." The Rabbit demonstrated an ebony locust twig, shaved off as skillfully as a knife could do it in the conventional rabbit fashion. The Deer found this solution appealing, so the Rabbit took a rough-edged hard stone and filed the Deer's teeth down until they were nearly worn to the gums.

"It hurts," said the Deer, but the Rabbit assured him that it always hurt a little when teeth started to get sharp, so the Deer endured silently.

"Now try it," finally said the Rabbit. The Deer attempted once more, but this time he couldn't bite at all.

"Now you've paid for your antlers," said the Rabbit, as he hopped away through the bushes. Since then, the Deer's teeth have remained blunt, and he can only chew on grass and leaves.

What Became Of The Rabbit

The Deer was deeply angered by the Rabbit's trick with his teeth and vowed to get revenge. However, he concealed his feelings and pretended to be friendly until he saw an opportunity. One day, as they were walking together and chatting, the Deer challenged the Rabbit to a jumping contest. Knowing the Rabbit's reputation as a great jumper, he proposed a test near a small stream by the path.

"Let's see if you can jump across this branch," said the Deer. "We'll go back a bit, and when I say Kû! we'll both run and jump."

The Rabbit agreed, and they went back to get a good starting point. When the Deer shouted Kû!, they both ran towards the stream. The Rabbit made a powerful leap and easily landed on the other side. But to his surprise, the Deer had used his trickery again and transformed the stream into a large river. The Rabbit couldn't cross back, and he remains on the other side to this day. The rabbit we know now is a small creature that came after the incident.

Why The Mink Smells

The Mink was known for being such a skilled thief that the animals finally decided to address the issue in a council. They reached a consensus to punish him by burning him. Thus, they captured the Mink, created a large fire, and threw him into it. As the flames rose and the smell of roasted flesh filled the air, they began to think that he had been punished enough and might reform his ways. Consequently, they rescued him from the fire.

However, the Mink was already burned black, and from that day on, he remained black in color. Furthermore, whenever he felt threatened or excited, he emitted a scent reminiscent of roasted meat. Despite this lesson, the Mink's behavior did not improve, and he continued to be an adept thief just as before.

Why The Mole Lives Underground

There was a man who was deeply in love with a woman, but she had no affection for him and rejected his advances. Despite his efforts to win her over, she remained disinterested, causing him great distress. In his despair, he fell sick, consumed by his thoughts about her. Along came the Mole, and upon finding him in such a despondent state, the Mole inquired about the reason for his sorrow. The man shared his heartrending tale, and upon hearing the whole story, the Mole said, "I can help you in such a way that not only will she come to like you but will willingly seek you out."

That very night, the Mole burrowed underground to where the woman was sound asleep in her bed and carefully removed her heart. Returning the same way, he handed her heart to the man, who could not see it even when it was placed in his hand. "Now, swallow her heart," the Mole instructed, "and she will be irresistibly drawn to come to you and won't be able to resist the attraction." The man swallowed her heart, and as the woman awoke, an unexplained longing for him filled her heart. She felt an inexplicable desire to be with him, as if she must seek him out immediately. Confused and unable to comprehend this newfound sentiment, considering she had never felt affection for him before, the feeling grew so intense that she was compelled to visit the man herself. She confessed her love for him and expressed her desire to be his wife. Consequently, they were married.

This sudden turn of events surprised all the magicians who were familiar with both of them. They wondered how such a transformation had occurred. Upon discovering the role of the Mole, whom they had previously dismissed as unimportant, they became envious and threatened to harm him. Fearing for his life, the Mole sought refuge underground and has never dared to emerge to the surface ever since.

The Terrapin's Escape From The Wolves

Once, the Possum and the Terrapin decided to go hunting for persimmons together. They found a tree abundant with ripe fruit, and the Possum climbed up to shake the persimmons down for the Terrapin. However, their peaceful gathering was interrupted when a wolf appeared and began snapping at the falling fruit before the Terrapin could reach it. Seizing an opportunity, the Possum managed to throw down an enormous persimmon (or some say a bone he carried with him), which lodged in the wolf's throat as he leaped for it, causing the wolf to choke to death.

The Terrapin had a clever idea and decided to use the wolf's ears as hominy spoons. He cut off the wolf's ears and carried them with him as he headed back home, leaving the Possum to continue enjoying the persimmons in the tree.

On his journey, the Terrapin encountered a house where he was invited to savor some kanahe'na gruel from a jar placed outside the door. He sat down near the jar and used one of the wolf's ears as a spoon to dip up the gruel. The sight of this peculiar utensil amazed the people of the house. After satisfying his hunger, he resumed his journey and came across another house where he was offered more kanahe'na. Once again, he used the wolf's ear as a spoon to eat his meal. Word spread quickly that the Terrapin had killed a wolf and was now using its ears as spoons.

All the wolves were furious and decided to capture the Terrapin. After catching him, they deliberated on what to do with him and finally agreed to boil him in a clay pot. But the Terrapin mocked their attempt, claiming he would kick the pot to pieces. They then planned to burn him in a fire, but the Terrapin laughed again, asserting that he could extinguish the fire. Frustrated, they resolved to throw him into the deepest part of the river and drown him. The Terrapin begged them not to do so, but they paid no heed, and threw him into the water.

Unbeknownst to the wolves, this was the Terrapin's plan all along. He quickly dove under the water, emerged on the other side, and managed to escape. Some accounts suggest that during the ordeal, the Terrapin's back was broken in several places. Nevertheless, he persevered and sang a healing song to mend his injuries:

Gû'daye'wû, Gû'daye'wû,

I have sewed myself together, I have sewed myself together,

And though the pieces came together, the scars remain on his shell to this day.

Inception Of The Groundhog Dance: The Groundhog's Head

Once, seven wolves captured a Groundhog and intended to kill it for a meal. However, the clever Groundhog proposed a different idea. He suggested that instead of killing him right away, they could partake in an exciting dance, inspired by the joyful Green-corn dance. The Groundhog explained that he would lean against seven trees in sequence, and as he sang a song, the wolves would dance out and then back in line at his signal. The final turn of the dance would determine which wolf could catch him and claim him as their prize.

The wolves, intrigued by the idea of learning a new dance, agreed to the Groundhog's proposal. The Groundhog began singing the first musical composition, Ha'wiye'ĕhĭ', and the wolves danced enthusiastically. They followed his signals and danced back and forth as he sang more compositions, moving from tree to tree. With each round of the dance, the Groundhog positioned himself closer to his hiding spot under a stump.

As the seventh musical composition began, the Groundhog informed the wolves that this would be the last dance, and they would chase him after his signal. He started the music, and the wolves danced ahead of him. When he signaled Yu!, he made a swift dash for his hiding spot. The wolves turned and chased after him, but he managed to reach his aperture first and dove in. The foremost wolf tried to catch him by the tail but only succeeded in breaking it off, leaving the Groundhog with a short tail ever since.

The Migration Of The Animals

During ancient times, when animals could communicate and hold meetings, and when Grubworm and Woodchuck used to marry humans, there occurred a severe famine of mast in the mountains. Concerned about their sustenance, all the animals and birds that relied on mast as their food source gathered for a council. They decided to send the Pigeon to scout the lowlands and determine if there was any available food. After a considerable period, the Pigeon returned with promising news, stating that she had discovered a region where the mast was so abundant that it reached "up to our ankles" on the ground.

Excited about this discovery, the animals and birds assembled as a large army and migrated down to the lowlands to find relief from the famine.

The Wolf's Revenge—The Wolf And The Dog

Kana'ti, having wolves as his skilled hunters, relied on them for various tasks. On one occasion, he dispatched two wolves simultaneously. One wolf ventured eastward but failed to return. Concerned for his missing companion, the second wolf, upon returning that night, sensed something was wrong and set out to find his fellow. After some time, he discovered his brother lying critically injured near a formidable green snake (sălikwâ'yĭ) that had attacked him. The snake, also gravely wounded, was unable to escape.

Filled with anger, the magic-endowed wolf plucked several hairs from his own whiskers and used them as projectiles, striking the snake's body and killing it instantly. He then hastened back to Kana'ti, who sent the Terrapin to summon a powerful healer residing in the west to attend to the injured wolf. However, knowing that the Terrapin was a slow traveler and that the medico needed time to prepare his healing remedies, the resourceful wolf used his magical abilities to mend his brother long before the healer arrived from the west.

The Ball Game Of The Birds And Animals

Once, there was a great ballplay challenge between the animals and the birds, and both sides agreed to participate. The animals, led by their formidable captain, the Bear, assembled on a grassy field near the river, while the birds perched in the treetops on the ridge, with the Eagle as their captain. The animals boasted of their strength, with the mighty Bear displaying his prowess by tossing logs along the way. The venerable Terrapin, known for his impenetrable shell, demonstrated his power by thumping heavily on the ground.

Among the birds was the swift Hawk, the majestic Tlă'nuwă, and the Eagle, all renowned for their flight abilities. As they were awaiting the commencement signal, two tiny creatures slightly larger than field mice approached the tree where the bird captain sat. They asked to join the game, but since they were four-footed, the Eagle questioned why they didn't join the animals instead. The creatures explained that they had tried, but the animals ridiculed and rejected them due to their small size. Moved by their plight, the birds decided to fashion wings for them.

Using pieces of leather from a drumhead, they created wings for one of the little animals, transforming it into Tla'mehă, the Bat. Impressed by the Bat's agility, the birds recognized him as one of their best players. As for the second animal, since they had no more leather, they decided to stretch its skin between its fore and hind feet, creating Tewa, the Flying Squirrel.

When the game commenced, the Flying Squirrel soared through the air, impressively carrying the ball from one tree to another. The birds skillfully kept the ball in the air until it dropped, and the Bat continued to dazzle with his flying maneuvers. The Bear and the Terrapin, despite their bravado, couldn't even get close to the ball. In the end, the birds secured victory, thanks to the Bat's adeptness in carrying the ball to the goal.

In appreciation for his exceptional ball preservation, the birds presented the Martin with a gourd for building his nest, a treasure he still cherishes to this day.

How The Turkey Got His Beard

After the Terrapin's surprising victory over the Rabbit in the race, the other animals were amazed and discussed it extensively. They had always considered the Terrapin slow, despite knowing that he possessed warrior skills and magical secrets. However, the Turkey remained unconvinced and believed there must be a trick behind the Terrapin's win. Determined to prove his point, Turkey decided to challenge the Terrapin.

One day, Turkey encountered the Terrapin on his way home from war, with a fresh scalp hanging from his neck and dragging on the ground. The Turkey found the sight amusing and commented, "That scalp doesn't suit you. Your neck is too short and low to wear it that way. Let me show you how to wear it properly."

The Terrapin agreed and handed the scalp to Turkey, who placed it around his neck. The Turkey then walked a short distance and asked the Terrapin how it looked. The Terrapin praised Turkey, saying it looked very nice and suited him well. The Turkey pretended to adjust the scalp in a different way and walked ahead again. Each time, the Terrapin complimented the Turkey on how good it looked.

However, Turkey had no intention of returning the scalp. Instead, he kept walking faster and eventually broke into a run, ignoring the Terrapin's pleas to return the scalp. Seeing that he couldn't catch the Turkey on foot, the Terrapin resorted to his conjuring art and used his bow to shoot cane splints into the Turkey's leg, crippling him. These splints became the numerous small bones in Turkey's leg, which served no practical purpose. Despite his efforts, the Terrapin couldn't catch Turkey, who continued to wear the scalp proudly around his neck.

Why The Turkey Gobbles

In the old days, ballplay was a favorite activity among the animals and birds, and the Grouse was known for his excellent voice and enthusiastic cheers during the game. Turkey, on the other hand, lacked a strong voice and sought the Grouse's help to improve. The Grouse agreed to teach him but asked for payment in the form of feathers to make a collar for himself. Thus, the Grouse acquired his collar made of turkey feathers.

During the lessons, the Turkey learned quickly, and the Grouse decided it was time to test his voice. He stood on a hollow log and signaled Turkey to shout as loudly as possible when he tapped on the log. However, the Turkey was so excited and eager that instead of shouting, he could only gobble. From that moment on, Turkey has been gobbling whenever he hears a noise.

How The Kingfisher Got His Bill

According to some elderly folks, in the beginning, the Kingfisher was intended to be a water bird, but without webbed feet or a suitable bill, he struggled to find sustenance. To address this, the animals convened a council and decided to fashion a bill resembling a long, sharp awl to serve as a fish-gig. Once equipped with the fish-gig, the Kingfisher flew to the top of a tree, gracefully soared over the water, and skillfully speared a fish with his gig. From that point forward, he became an expert fish-gigger.

Another version suggests that a Blacksnake discovered a Yellowhammer's nest in a hollow tree, consuming the young birds and coiling up to rest in the nest. Upon returning, the mother bird sought help from the Little People, who directed her to the Kingfisher. Flying back and forth in front of the tree's opening, the Kingfisher finally swooped down and swiftly eliminated the snake. The Little People observed that the Kingfisher used a thin, sharp fish called tugălû'nă, which he carried in his bill like a lance, to perforate an opening in the snake's head. Impressed by his skill, they rewarded him with the long bill he now possesses, knowing he would excel as a gigger.

How The Partridge Got His Whistle

In ancient times, the Terrapin possessed a splendid whistle, while the Partridge had none. The Terrapin often flaunted his whistle to the other animals, which stirred jealousy in the Partridge. One day, the Partridge asked the Terrapin for permission to give it a try. Though hesitant at first, fearing a trick, the Terrapin finally agreed, and the Partridge assured him that he would return the whistle right away. To build trust, the Partridge suggested the Terrapin stay with him during practice.

As the Partridge practiced, the Terrapin accompanied him, offering positive feedback. The Partridge then showed off his whistling while running a bit faster. The Terrapin praised his skill but advised him not to run too fast. Undeterred, the Partridge asked the Terrapin's opinion once more and, with a grand gesture, spread his wings, emitted a long, beautiful whistle, and gracefully flew to the top of a tree, leaving the astonished Terrapin far below.

Regrettably, the Terrapin never recovered his whistle, and after losing his scalp to Turkey as well, he became too embarrassed to be seen and began hiding in his shell when approached by anyone. As a result, he has remained silent in his shell ever since.

How The Redbird Got His Color

One day, a Raccoon crossed paths with a Wolf and began insulting him with hurtful remarks. The Wolf grew angry and started chasing the Raccoon. The Raccoon ran swiftly and reached a tree by the riverside before the Wolf caught up. Climbing the tree, he perched on a limb that extended over the water. Seeing the reflection in the water, the Wolf thought it was the Raccoon and lunged at it. He ended up nearly drowning before managing to climb out, soaked and dripping.

As the Wolf lay on the riverbank, trying to dry himself and recovering from the ordeal, he fell asleep. Seizing the opportunity, the Raccoon sneaked down the tree and smeared the Wolf's eyes with dung. When the Wolf awoke, he found his eyes sealed shut and started whimpering in distress. Along came a little brown bird, who heard the Wolf's cries and inquired about the matter. The Wolf explained the situation and added, "If you help me open my eyes, I'll show you where to find beautiful red paint to adorn yourself."

The compassionate brown bird agreed, pecking gently at the Wolf's eyes until the plaster was removed, allowing him to see again. In gratitude, the Wolf led the bird to a rock with streaks of brilliant red paint. The little bird painted himself with the red paint and has been known as the Redbird ever since.

The Race Between The Crane And The Hummingbird

Both the Hummingbird and the Crane were enamored with a beautiful woman. She favored the Hummingbird for his striking appearance, while finding the Crane unattractive and cumbersome. However, the Crane was persistent, and in order to get rid of him, the woman finally declared that he must challenge the Hummingbird to a race, and she would marry the winner. Believing the Hummingbird's speed would ensure his victory, she did not know the Crane could fly through the night.

They agreed to start from the woman's house and fly around the world, and the one who returned first would win her hand. As soon as the race began, the Hummingbird shot off like a lightning bolt, disappearing from sight in an instant, leaving the Crane to lumber behind. The Hummingbird flew all day, resting at night, and by morning, he was well ahead. However, the Crane flew steadily through the night, passing the Hummingbird just after midnight, and resting by a creek until daybreak while spearing tadpoles for breakfast.

The Hummingbird was surprised to find the Crane ahead but continued on, thinking he would easily catch up. The Crane maintained his lead, passing the Hummingbird again on the fourth and fifth days, and by the seventh day, he was a full night's journey ahead. The Crane arrived back at the woman's house early in the morning, freshening up before his arrival. When the Hummingbird reached her in the afternoon, he realized he had lost the race. However, the woman declared she could never marry someone as unattractive as the Crane, and so she remained single.

The Owl Gets Married

A widow with a daughter always emphasized the importance of marrying a good hunter to her young girl. The daughter listened attentively and promised to heed her mother's advice. Eventually, a suitor came to seek the girl's hand, but the widow informed him that only a skilled hunter could marry her daughter. "I am precisely that kind of man," said the suitor, persisting in his request. He asked the mother to speak on his behalf to the young woman. So the mother told her daughter about the young man who had come courting and claimed to be a proficient hunter, encouraging her to consider him. "As you wish," replied the daughter. And thus, the arrangement was made, and the young man moved in with the girl.

The following morning, he declared his intent to go hunting but abruptly changed his mind, opting to go fishing instead. He spent the entire day away from home and returned late at night with only three small fish, claiming that he had no luck but promising better results the next day. The pattern repeated when he went fishing again the next day, returning with only two insignificant lizards and using the same excuse. On the third day, he said he would go hunting, but he came back with only a handful of scraps that he had found where other hunters had already processed a deer.

The widow grew suspicious by this point. Therefore, she instructed her daughter to secretly follow the young man and observe his actions. The daughter trailed him through the woods and kept him in sight until he reached the riverbank. There, she saw him transform into a hooting owl and fly over to a pile of driftwood in the water, crying, "U-gu-ku! hu! hu! u! u!" She was both surprised and furious, thinking to herself, "I thought I married a man, but my husband is only an owl." The daughter watched as the owl searched the water and eventually brought up a crawfish in his talons. He then reverted to his human form, carrying the crawfish, and started heading home. The daughter hurried ahead through the woods and arrived home before him. When he came in with the crawfish in his hand, she questioned him about the fish he had caught. He claimed that the owl had frightened them all away. "I think you are the owl," she accused, and promptly sent him out of the house. The owl retreated into the woods, where he pined away in sorrow and love, until there was no flesh left on his body except his head.

The Huhu Gets Married

A widow with only a daughter, but no son, faced considerable challenges in making a living. She constantly emphasized to her young daughter the need for a man in the family who could be a skilled worker and assist in various tasks. One evening, a stranger arrived, expressing his interest in courting the young woman. When the girl mentioned that she could only marry someone who was a hard worker, the suitor confidently claimed to be just such a man. The daughter discussed this with her mother, and they decided to get married based on his assurance.

The next morning, the widow handed her new son-in-law a hoe and directed him to work in the cornfield. When breakfast was ready, she went to call him, following the sound of someone hoeing on stony ground. However, upon reaching the spot, she found only a small area of hoed ground, and there was no sign of her son-in-law. In the distance, she heard a huhu bird calling.

He didn't return for lunch either, and when he finally came home in the evening, the widow asked where he had been all day. He confidently replied that he had been hard at work. Satisfied with his response, they had supper together.

The next morning, he left again with the hoe over his shoulder. When breakfast was ready, the widow went to call him, but once more, there was no sign of him doing any work. Only the hoe lay there, and nothing had been accomplished. In the distance, a huhu bird was calling as before.

Upon his return in the evening, the widow inquired about his activities that day. The man confidently claimed he had been working hard. However, the widow was perplexed, as he hadn't been at the site when she called him. He explained that he had gone to the thicket briefly to visit some relatives. The widow responded, noting that the swamp was inhabited only by huhu birds and that her daughter needed a diligent and hardworking husband, not a lazy huhu. She declared that he must leave their home.

Why The Buzzard's Head Is Bare

Once, the buzzard had a magnificent topknot that he cherished and took great pride in. He was so enamored with his appearance that he refused to eat carrion like the other birds. While his fellow birds feasted on the carcass of a deer or some other animal they had discovered, he would strut around, boasting, "You may have it all, it is beneath me."

The other birds decided to teach him a lesson and devised a plan with the help of the buffalo. They not only took away the buzzard's topknot but also removed almost all the other feathers on his head. This incident humbled the buzzard greatly, and he lost his former pride. Consequently, he now willingly consumes carrion for his sustenance.

The Eagle's Revenge

Once, a hunter residing in the mountains heard a peculiar noise during the night, resembling a rushing wind, just outside his cabin. Curious about the source of the sound, he ventured out and discovered an eagle perched on the drying pole, tearing at the body of a deer hanging there. Without considering the consequences, the hunter impulsively shot the eagle.

The following morning, he took the deer back to the settlement and shared his deed with the chief. In response, the chief sent some men to retrieve the dead eagle and prepare for an Eagle dance. The men brought back the lifeless eagle, and preparations were swiftly made for the dance in the townhouse.

As the night advanced, around midnight, a strange warrior arrived at the dance circle, recounting his valorous exploits. No one recognized him, assuming he hailed from a distant Cherokee town. He narrated how he had taken a life, and at the culmination of each tale, he emitted a hoarse yell, "Hi!" that startled the entire assembly. Tragically, one of the seven men with rattles fell over dead due to the shock. Undeterred, the stranger continued singing and sharing his deeds, and with each yell, another rattler met the same fate. The people were paralyzed with fear, unable to move from their positions.

Unrelenting, the stranger persisted until all seven rattlers had succumbed, and then he vanished into the darkness. It was later revealed by the hunter who shot the eagle that the warrior was, in fact, the brother of the eagle he had killed.

The Hunter And The Buzzard

After an entire day of fruitless hunting for deer in the mountains, the hunter, feeling thoroughly exhausted, decided to take a break and sat down on a log to rest and contemplate his next move. Just then, a buzzard, a bird known for its magical abilities, flew overhead and initiated a conversation with him. The buzzard inquired about the hunter's troubles, and upon hearing his story, it suggested a solution. The buzzard informed the hunter that there were plenty of deer on the ridges beyond, but they could only be seen from high up in the air. It proposed an exchange of forms, where the hunter would transform into a buzzard and fly over the mountain to locate the deer, while the buzzard would take on the hunter's human form and go home to his wife.

The tired hunter agreed to the proposal, and the transformation took place. The buzzard became a man and went home to the hunter's wife, who welcomed him, mistaking him for her husband. Meanwhile, the hunter, now in the form of a buzzard, soared over the mountain to search for deer. After spending some time with the woman, the buzzard excused himself, explaining that he needed to go out and find game to sustain them. Returning to the location where the hunter had first encountered the buzzard, the transformed hunter was waiting patiently.

Upon reuniting, the buzzard asked the hunter about his success, and the hunter happily revealed that he had indeed found several deer, just as the buzzard had predicted. The buzzard restored the hunter to his human shape, and in return, it transformed back into its original buzzard form and flew away. From that day onward, the hunter never returned empty-handed from his hunting expeditions, as he had learned the secret of finding deer in the mountains from the magical buzzard.

The UKTENA And The ULÛÑSÛ'TĬ

In ancient times, when the Sun grew angry with the people on Earth and sent a devastating sickness upon them, the Little Men decided to transform a man into a monstrous snake called Uktena, known as "The Keen-eyed," and send him to defeat the sickness. However, Uktena failed in his mission, and the Rattlesnake had to be sent instead. This failure made Uktena jealous and enraged, causing people to fear him. He was then taken up to Gălûñ'lătĭ to reside with other dangerous creatures. Yet, there are other creatures like him that lurk in deep pools in the river and solitary passes in the high mountains, known as "Where the Uktena stays" by the Cherokee.

Those who are familiar with the legend describe the Uktena as an enormous snake, as thick as a tree trunk, with horns on its head and a dazzling crest like a diamond on its forehead. Its scales shimmer like sparks of fire, adorned with rings or spots of vibrant colors along its length. Only the seventh spot from its head is vulnerable, as it houses its heart and life. The blazing diamond on its forehead, known as Ulûñsû'tĭ or "Transparent," grants great powers to whoever possesses it, making them the most accomplished wonder worker in the tribe. However, attempting to acquire it is perilous, as whoever the Uktena sets eyes upon becomes entranced by the radiant light and unwittingly approaches the snake instead of fleeing. Even witnessing the Uktena asleep brings death, not to the observer, but to their entire family.

Only one brave warrior, găn-uni'tsĭ, succeeded in finding the Ulûñsû'tĭ and returned. The East Cherokee still preserve the crystal he brought back—a large transparent crystal with a blood-red streak running through its center. It is securely kept wrapped in a deerskin, hidden inside an earthen jar concealed in a secret mountain cave. Every seven days, the owner feeds it with the blood of small animals, rubbing the blood on the crystal after each kill. Twice a year, it requires the blood of a large animal like a deer. Should the owner forget to feed it, the crystal may emerge from its cave in the form of fire, flying through the air to quench its thirst with the lifeblood of the conjurer or one of their kin. The conjurer can prevent this by informing the crystal, before putting it away, that it will not be needed for a long time. It will then fall into a dormant slumber, feeling no hunger until it is needed again.

The Ulûñsû'tĭ is never to be shown to a white man or anyone else, as it is believed that any person other than the owner who looks upon it will suffer sudden death. Even the conjurer who possesses it is fearful of its power and frequently changes its hiding place to prevent the crystal from learning the way out. When the conjurer passes away, the crystal will be buried with them; otherwise, it will emerge like a blazing star and search for the grave night after night for seven years, finally returning to eternal slumber where it was placed.

The possessor of the Ulûñsû'tĭ is assured prosperity in hunting, love, rain-making, and all endeavors. Its most significant use is in prophecy, as the crystal reflects the future like a tree mirrored in a calm stream. The conjurer can discern whether a sick person will recover, if a warrior will return from battle, or if a young person will live to old age by consulting the crystal.

ÂGĂN-UNI'TSĬ's Search For The UKTENA

In one of their battles with the Shawano, a tribe of powerful magicians, the Cherokee captured a renowned medicine-man known as găn-uni'tsĭ, or "The Ground-hogs' Mother." While they had him ready for torture, he pleaded for his life and promised to find for them the great wonder worker, the Ulûñsû'tĭ. This marvel was believed to be a blazing star set in the forehead of the formidable Uktena serpent, and possessing it would grant incredible powers. However, meeting the Uktena was certain death, and everyone warned găn-uni'tsĭ of the peril. Undeterred, he insisted that his medicine was strong, and he was not afraid. The Cherokee spared his life on the condition that he would embark on the search for the Ulûñsû'tĭ.

Setting forth, the magician ventured to various gaps in the mountain range. At each location, he encountered massive serpents and other formidable creatures, but none were the Ulûñsû'tĭ. Mocking those who were terrified, he continued southward in his quest. Eventually, he reached Gahû'tĭ mountain, where he found the Uktena asleep. Acting quickly, găn-uni'tsĭ shot the serpent through its heart, avoiding its deadly gaze. The Uktena, now awakened, pursued him, but the magician used his cunning and agility to escape its wrath.

Returning to the bottom of the mountain, găn-uni'tsĭ created a circle of fire using pine cones and dug a trench within it. The Uktena's poison could not pass the circle, and the dying serpent's blood ran into the trench, leaving the magician unharmed. The birds in the woods gathered to feast on the Uktena's remains, leaving nothing behind, not even the bones.

After seven days, găn-uni'tsĭ went back to the spot and found the diamond from the Uktena's head resting on a low-hanging branch. He carefully wrapped it up and took it with him, becoming the most esteemed medicine-man in the tribe.

Returning to the settlement, the people noticed a small snake hanging from găn-uni'tsĭ's head where the drop of poison had struck him, but he remained unaware of its presence throughout his life.

The trench filled with the Uktena's blood became a dark lake where women would later dye cane splits for their baskets.

The Red Man And The UKTENA

Two brothers embarked on a hunting trip together. When they reached a suitable camping spot in the mountains, they lit a fire. While one brother gathered bark to build a shelter, the other decided to explore up the creek in search of a deer. Suddenly, he heard a commotion on the ridge, like two animals engaged in a fierce battle. Intrigued, he hastened through the bushes to investigate. To his astonishment, he discovered a massive uktena, a dangerous serpent, coiled around a man and strangling him to death. The desperate man cried out to the hunter, identifying him as his nephew and imploring for help, stating that the uktena was an enemy to both of them. The hunter aimed carefully, drew his arrow, and released it with precision, hitting the uktena's body, causing blood to spew from the wound. The snake released its grip and rolled down the ridge, creating havoc in the valley.

The man who was saved turned out to be Asga'ya Gi'gǎgeǐ, the Red Man of the Lightning. He expressed his gratitude to the hunter for aiding him and promised a reward—a special medicine to ensure the hunter's success in finding game always. After nightfall, they descended to the spot where the uktena had perished. However, the body was consumed by birds and insects, leaving only the bones. The Red Man noticed flashes of light emanating from the ground and unearthed a single scale of the uktena just below the surface. He then gathered splinters from a lightning-struck tree, ignited a fire, and burnt the uktena scale to a coal. Wrapping it in a piece of deerskin, he bestowed it upon the hunter, declaring that as long as he kept it, he would be able to easily kill game.

The Red Man further advised the hunter to hang the potent medicine on a tree outside the camp since it was perilous. He also foretold that upon returning to the cabin, the hunter's brother would be gravely ill due to the presence of the uktena's scale. To heal him, the Red Man provided the hunter with a bit of cane and instructed him to scrape a small portion into water and give it to his brother to drink. Following the Red Man's guidance, the hunter nursed his brother back to health, and from that day onwards, whenever he went hunting, he always found plentiful game.

The Hunter And The UKSU'HĬ

A man residing in Georgia decided to visit his relatives at Hickory-log. Being a skilled hunter, he planned to venture into the mountains. However, his friends cautioned him against heading north, as there was a dangerous and massive uksu'hĭ snake near a large uprooted tree in that direction. This treacherous serpent would ambush unsuspecting hunters, coil around them, and squeeze the life out of them before dragging their lifeless bodies down the mountain into a deep crevice in Hiwassee.

Though he listened carefully to the warning, the man's curiosity got the better of him, and he secretly set off on his journey, heading straight up the mountain toward the north. As he approached the fallen tree, he noticed the enormous uksu'hĭ lying in the grass with its head raised, but looking away. Terrified, he immediately climbed down and began to run. The snake heard the noise and swiftly pursued him. Up the ridge and down the other side toward the river, the man sprinted, but the uksu'hĭ closed in rapidly. Finally, it caught up with him, coiling around him and trapping one arm while leaving the other free.

The uksu'hĭ exerted a painful constriction that nearly broke the man's ribs and started dragging him toward the water. In desperation, he grasped at the bushes they passed, but the snake blew its nauseating breath into his face, forcing him to let go. As they neared a deep crevice by the river, the hunter had a fortunate idea. He was drenched in sweat from the arduous run across the mountain and remembered that snakes despised the smell of perspiration. So, he quickly reached into his bosom, gathering sweat from under his armpit on his hand. When the uksu'hĭ turned its head, he swiftly slapped his sweaty hand on the snake's nasal sensor.

The uksu'hĭ let out a gasp, as if wounded, and released its coils, swiftly gliding away through the bushes. The hunter, though bruised, managed to make his way back home to Hickory-log, relieved to have escaped the perilous encounter with the formidable snake.

The USTÛ'TLĬ

Long ago, there dwelled a fearsome serpent known as the Ustû'tlĭ on Cohutta mountain. Unlike other snakes, it possessed feet at each end of its body, enabling it to move in jerky strides like a large worm. Its triangular, flat feet clung to the ground like suckers, granting it the ability to raise itself on its hind feet and reach for fresh holds. With its snaky head held high, it could traverse rivers and ravines by swinging its body over.

The Ustû'tlĭ was a perilous creature, and wherever its footprints were found, danger lurked. Its bleating cries, similar to those of a young fawn, caused hunters to flee in the opposite direction. No one dared to venture near Cohutta mountain due to the Ustû'tlĭ's menacing presence.

However, a man from a northern settlement came to visit his relatives in that area. When they could only offer him a meal of corn and beans, explaining that the hunters were too afraid to go into the mountains, he bravely decided to face the Ustû'tlĭ himself. Despite their attempts to dissuade him, he remained determined and agreed to heed their advice about the fawn bleats and the direction to run if pursued.

The following morning, he set out toward the mountain and, pushing through the underbrush, heard the unmistakable sound of a fawn bleating. Convinced that it was the Ustû'tlĭ, he pressed forward and encountered the monstrous serpent with its head held high, scanning the surroundings for prey. Spotting the hunter, the snake immediately advanced, using its jerky strides to close the distance.

Terrified, the hunter initially ran straight up the mountain. However, recalling the warning, he altered his course and ran along the side of the ridge. This maneuver caused the Ustû'tlĭ to lose ground as it struggled to maintain balance. The hunter continued until he reached the crest of the ridge, leaving the snake out of sight.

He then descended to the base of the mountain and set the grass and leaves ablaze, surrounding the Ustû'tlĭ with fire. Desperate to escape, the serpent sought refuge on a high cliff, but the flames followed relentlessly. As the Ustû'tlĭ tried to spring across the wall of fire, it succumbed to the choking smoke, losing its grip and falling among the burning pine trunks until it was reduced to ashes.